CW00871904

Anne of Green Gables

By L. M. Montgomery

A new version of the
favorite children classic
by Archie Oliver

HINKLER
BOOKS

Anne of Green Gables
First published in 2003 by
Hinkler Books Pty Ltd
17–23 Redwood Drive
Dingley VIC 3172 Australia
www.hinklerbooks.com

© Hinkler Books Pty Ltd 2003

10 9 8 7 6 5 4
10 09 08 07

ISBN 1 8651 5583 7

Editor: Heather Hammonds
Cover Illustration: Terry Riley
Illustrations: Mike Lacey
Typesetting: Midland Typesetters
Printed & bound in Australia

The Author
Lucy Maud Montgomery

Lucy Maud Montgomery (1874–1942) was born on Canada's Prince Edward Island. The island was the setting for Anne of Green Gables and nine other "Anne" books.

Every year, a quarter of a million tourists visit the island to see the places that inspired Lucy Maud Montgomery's hugely popular stories.

There are many similarities between the author's life and her world-famous character, the orphan Anne.

Montgomery was an only child, and her own mother died when she was two. She was sent to live with her strict grandparents, on a farm on the island.

She later qualified as a teacher, married a church minister and had her own family.

After her death, Lucy Maud Montgomery was buried next to the house on which she based Green Gables.

Contents

Chapter 1
Astonishing News

"We're going to adopt a boy from the orphanage," announced Marilla, as she and her neighbor Rachel were having afternoon tea together. "Matthew's gone to the station to pick him up right now."

If Marilla Cuthbert had said that her brother Matthew had gone to Australia to meet a kangaroo, Rachel could not have been more astonished

Marilla and Matthew were both almost sixty years old, and had lived at Green Gables together for most of their lives.

Rachel was struck dumb with the news. A boy! Marilla and Matthew Cuthbert of all people adopting a boy! The world had turned upside down.

"What on earth put such an idea in your head?" Rachel demanded to know, when she recovered her wits. "You don't know anything about children. There's never been a child at

Green Gables. You're bringing a strange boy to your house and you don't know a thing about him. Don't say I didn't warn you when he burns the homestead down and puts poison in the well."

Marilla, a tall thin woman with her dark hair twisted up into a hard little knot behind her head, answered as though getting an orphan was an everyday experience. "I think it's a good idea. A boy can help Matthew on the farm. Matthew's getting old and he's not as fit as he was."

Rachel may have been astonished at the news. But if she could have seen who was waiting at the railway station at that very moment, she would have been more surprised than ever.

*

Matthew Cuthbert tied his horse and buggy to a post, and walked onto the station platform.

There was no sign of the train. The platform was almost deserted. The only living thing to be seen was a little girl sitting alone on a bench.

Matthew, perhaps the shyest man alive, dreaded all women except Marilla. He had an uncomfortable feeling that the mysterious creatures were secretly laughing at him.

He may have been quite right, for he was an odd-looking character, with a lanky figure, gray hair that touched his stooping shoulders, and a soft gray beard.

Matthew went to find the stationmaster, walking straight past the girl without saying a word.

He found the stationmaster in his office. "When's the train due?" he asked.

"We're going to adopt a boy."

"Been and gone, Matthew, it was early," said the stationmaster. "But there was a passenger dropped off for you – a little girl. That's her on the bench."

"I'm not expecting a girl," said Matthew, a little confused. "I've come for a boy."

"Then I guess someone's made a mistake," answered the stationmaster. "The person who left her just said she was a girl you'd adopted, and you'd pick her up. I certainly haven't got any more orphans hidden about the station!"

Matthew stood with a stunned look on his face. "I don't understand," he mumbled.

"Best ask the girl," suggested the stationmaster. "She's got a tongue of her own, that's for sure."

Matthew now had no choice. He had to walk up to a girl – a strange orphan girl – and ask her why she wasn't a boy!

Matthew is confused.

Chapter 2
The Little Orphan Girl

There was no escape. Matthew shuffled down the platform towards the girl.

She was a child of about eleven and dressed in a well-worn, yellow cotton dress. She had a straw hat on her head, and from beneath it tumbled two thick braids of bright red hair.

The girl's face was small, white and thin, and covered with freckles. Matthew was both surprised and much relieved when she spoke first.

"I suppose you're Matthew Cuthbert," she said, in a particularly sweet and clear voice. "I'm glad to see you. I was beginning to think you weren't coming."

Matthew was about to say something, when the girl started talking again.

"I was imagining all the things that might have prevented you from coming," she said. "I had made up my mind that if you didn't come, I'd go down the track to that beautiful big cherry tree and climb up into it, to sleep for

"I suppose you're Matthew Cuthbert."

the night. I wouldn't be a bit afraid, and it would be lovely to sleep in a wild cherry tree, all white with bloom in the moonshine, don't you think? You could imagine you were sleeping in a great room decorated with wonderful flowers."

Matthew took a few moments to recover from the sudden explosion of words that rushed from the girl's mouth.

The first thing he decided was that *he* wasn't going to be the one to tell her he was expecting a boy. He would take her back to Green Gables. Marilla could sort out the problem.

"I'm sorry I'm late," he mumbled shyly. "Come along. The horse is in the yard. Give me your bag."

There was an ancient old canvas bag at her feet

"Oh, I can carry that," smiled the girl. "It isn't heavy. I've got all my worldly goods in it. And if it isn't carried in a certain way, the handle falls off. So I'd better carry it because I've got the knack of it. Oh, I am glad you came for me, even if it would have been nice to sleep in the wild cherry tree. Besides I love driving in a buggy."

The girl continued to talk, as they left the platform.

"Oh, it seems so wonderful that I'm going to

The Little Orphan Girl

"Oh, I am glad you came for me."

live with you and belong to you. I've never belonged to anybody before. I don't suppose you were ever an orphan, were you? You can't possible imagine how awful it is.

"Being an orphan is worse than anything you can imagine. Though, it was nice to imagine about the other girls in the orphanage – to imagine that the girl beside me was the daughter of an earl, who had been stolen away from her parents by a cruel nurse who died the night before she could confess her crime.

"I used to lie awake all night and imagine things like that. I guess that's why I am so thin. I am dreadfully thin, aren't I? There isn't a drop of fat on me. Some times, I love to imagine I'm nice and plump with dimples in my elbows."

With that, the little orphan girl stopped talking – she was out of breath.

Matthew's head was spinning with hearing so many words all at once.

Chapter 3
Green Gables

The little girl was silent for a few moments, as Matthew helped her into the buggy and they began the journey home.

He hardly had time to say "gee-up" to the horse before she began to talk again.

"Did you see that tree we just passed? Wasn't it beautiful! The blossom is all white and lacey. It's like a wedding dress. I love pretty clothes. I've never had a pretty dress in my life. But then it's something I can look forward to, isn't it? And I can always imagine I am wearing a pretty dress. Today I'm wearing a horrid old cotton dress, but really I imagine it's a beautiful, pale blue silk gown."

Matthew shook his head and wondered if she would ever stop talking.

The girl took a quick breath, before continuing. "Am I talking too much? People are always telling me I do. Would you rather I didn't talk? If you say so, I'll stop."

Matthew, much to his surprise, was actually starting to enjoy himself. Like most quiet folks, he liked talkative people who didn't expect him to say anything.

"Oh, you can talk as much as you like," he replied. "I don't mind."

"I'm so glad," she said. "I know you and I are going to get along fine together. It's such a relief to talk when one wants to, and not to be told that children should be seen and not heard. People laugh at me sometimes because I use big words. But if you have big ideas, you have to use big words to express them, don't you?"

"That seems reasonable," said Matthew.

Suddenly, the girl started on a different subject. "Your place is called Green Gables, isn't it? I was told there were trees all around it. I just love trees. There weren't any at the orphanage, only a few tiny plants.

"They might have grown big, happy and healthy in the wild with the other trees and flowers. But they couldn't. They were trapped in the orphanage, just like me. I felt sorry to leave them today. But I comforted myself by thinking that there might be a babbling brook at Green Gables."

"There's one right below the house," said Matthew.

"Oh, it's been my dream to live near a brook!" cried the girl. "But dreams don't often come true, do they? Wouldn't it be nice if they did? Right now I feel almost perfectly happy. But then, I could never be perfectly happy. Nobody with red hair could be. I don't mind my freckles, green eyes and my skinniness. I can imagine those away, but I can never imagine away my red hair. I try to imagine it as black as

Blossom all white and lacey

a raven's wing but I can't. My red hair will be my lifelong sorrow."

Just then, the horse and buggy topped the rise and the girl looked down at the valley below.

A river was winding through the middle of it. The water was glinting in the last rays of the setting sun. A small wooden bridge crossed the river.

There were a few isolated homes on both sides of the valley.

Near the bridge, a stream led off from the river to fill a huge pond. The girl heard the sweet chorus of croaking frogs echoing from its edges.

"That's Barry's Pond," said Matthew.

"Why do they call it that?" asked the girl.

"Because it's on Mr. Barry's farm."

"I don't like that name," said the girl. "It's such a beautiful pond. I shall call it the Lake of Shining Waters."

Matthew smiled as the girl's imagination. "Look!" he said suddenly, pointing up the valley side to a house that stood on the edge of a wood.

"Oh, don't tell me," she said breathlessly. "Let me guess. That's Green Gables, isn't it!"

"That's Green Gables, isn't it!"

"So it is," said Matthew. "You sound as though you've seen it before."

"No. I had no idea what it looked like but as soon as I saw it, I felt it was home. It's like a dream. You've no idea how many times I've pinched myself today to make sure everything isn't a dream. Now I know it's real. That is Green Gables and we're nearly home."

Matthew felt uneasy. He was glad it was his sister Marilla who would have to tell the girl that maybe the home she dreamed of was not to be hers after all.

The horse buggy turned into the yard as the poplar trees all around started rustling in the evening breeze.

"Listen to the trees talking in their sleep," said the girl. "What nice dreams they must be having."

Chapter 4
A Dreadful Situation

Marilla Cuthbert saw her brother Matthew coming through the front door of Green Gables, followed by the little girl with red hair.

"Matthew Cuthbert," she said, with a look of surprise on her face. "Where's the boy?"

"There wasn't any boy at the station," he answered, feeling quite awful about the whole thing. "There was only a girl there."

He suddenly realized he had not even asked the girl what her name was.

"No boy!" exclaimed Marilla. "But there must have been a boy!"

"There wasn't," said Matthew defensively. "The station master said that only a girl came on the train."

Marilla scratched her head.

"You don't want me!" the girl suddenly cried. "You don't want me because I'm not a boy! I might have expected it. Nobody ever wanted me. I might have known it was all too beautiful to last."

With that, she threw herself on a sofa, buried her face in her arms and burst into tears.

Marilla and Matthew were at a loss for words.

"Come now," said Marilla at last, "there's no need for tears."

The little girl raised her tear-stained face and then took a big breath. "Yes, there is. You would cry too, if you were an orphan. You'd cry if you came to a place you thought was going to be home and found out they didn't want you because you weren't a boy. This is the most tragical thing that ever happened to me."

Marilla had never heard a young girl use such a strange word before. "Now, now," she said, "don't cry. We are not going to throw you out of doors tonight. You can stay until we have time to investigate how the mistake happened. Now, first of all, what is your name?"

"Please call me Cordelia," said the girl, calming down a little.

"Is that your name?" asked Marilla.

"Not exactly," answered the girl, "but I would love to be called Cordelia. It's such a pretty name."

A Dreadful Situation

"You don't want me!"

Anne of Green Gables

Marilla was more confused than ever. "If Cordelia isn't your name, what is it?"

"Anne Shirley," was the reluctant answer, "but oh, please call me Cordelia. It can't matter what you call me if I'm only going to be here for a little while. Anne is such an unromantic name."

"Fiddlesticks!" said Marilla. "Anne is a sensible name. It's nothing to be ashamed about."

"I'm not ashamed of it," explained Anne, "only I like Cordelia better. I always imagined I was called Cordelia, although when I was very young I imagined myself as Geraldine. But now it's Cordelia. But if you must call me Anne, please call me Anne spelled with an *e*. It looks so much better spelled with an *e*.

It was all too much for Marilla. "I don't know how I call you Anne with an *e*. But if it pleases you, your name is Anne with an *e*."

Even with that problem solved, Marilla could find no explanation why a girl rather than a boy had turned up.

"Matthew and I wanted a boy to help us on the farm," she explained to Anne. "A girl is not much use to us."

With that, Marilla set the table for supper and served up the meat pie she had prepared earlier.

"I can't eat," sighed Anne. "I can never eat when I am in the depths of despair. Can you eat when you are feeling so awful?"

"I've never been in the depths of despair," answered Marilla.

Later, Marilla put Anne to bed upstairs. The girl quickly hid herself beneath the bedclothes.

"Now you try and sleep," said Marilla, as kindly as she could. "Good night."

In an instant, Anne's head appeared again. "How can you call it a good night?" she asked. "This must be the worst night I have ever had!"

Then she dived beneath the bedclothes again.

Marilla went downstairs. "Well, this is a dreadful situation," she said to Matthew. "She'll have to go back to the orphanage."

"She's a nice little thing," said Matthew. "It would be kind of sad to send her back when she's so set on staying here."

"What good would she be to us?" asked Marilla.

Matthew shook his head. "Perhaps we might be some good to her."

"I think the child's bewitched you," replied Marilla.

"I just think she's an interesting little thing.

In the depths of despair

You should have heard her talking on the ride back from the station."

"Oh, she can talk fast enough," said Marilla. "She can't stop talking! No! She's got to go back."

And that was the last word on it that night. Marilla and Matthew went to their bedrooms.

Close by, a lonely, friendless child cried herself to sleep.

Chapter 5

First Morning at Green Gables

Sunshine was flooding into Anne's room when she awoke the next day.

For a moment, she could not remember where she was. Then came a delightful thrill of something pleasant, followed by a terrible thought. This was Green Gables. And no one wanted her because she was a girl!

Anne got out of bed and kneeled at the window, looking out at the beautiful summer morning.

Below her window, a lush green meadow ran down to the sparkling brook. Beyond that lay the river. And on the other side was her Lake of Shining Waters.

She looked to the left, and saw houses and barns in the distance. And way beyond them, she caught a glimpse of the sparkling blue sea.

Anne had seen so many ugly and unhappy

Looking out at the beautiful summer morning

sights in her young life. What she saw now was as lovely as anything she had ever dreamed of, or imagined.

Anne's thoughts were interrupted when Marilla came into the room. "It's time you were dressed," she said sharply.

Marilla didn't really know how to talk to a child. She had become too used to living alone with Matthew. So she sounded sharp, even when she didn't really mean to.

"Oh, isn't this all wonderful," said Anne, pointing out of the window.

Marilla was about to answer when Anne began one of her breathless speeches.

"The garden. The orchard. The woods. The whole world. The world loves us all today, don't you think? I can hear the brook laughing. Have you ever noticed what cheerful things brooks are? They're always laughing. Even in winter, I've heard them laughing beneath the ice. I'm so glad there's a brook near Green Gables.

"Perhaps you think it doesn't matter to me when I'm not going to be allowed to stay here. But it does. I shall always remember it, even if I never see it again. If there weren't a brook I would be haunted by a horrible feeling that there ought to be one.

"I'm not in the depths of despair this morning. I never can be in the morning. Isn't it wonderful that there are things like mornings? But I am feeling sad. I have just been imagining that you really wanted me to stay for ever and ever. But even I have to stop imagining things sometimes. And that's when I get sad."

Anne gasped and took a breath. Marilla took her chance to say a word. "Never mind your imaginings," she said, "just get dressed. Breakfast is waiting."

Anne washed, dressed and brushed her hair neatly before going downstairs. "I'm quite hungry this morning," she announced.

But before Marilla could ask her what she wanted to eat, Anne took a deep breath and was off again.

"I'm so glad the sun is shining. The world doesn't seem such a confusing place this morning. But I like rainy mornings very well too. All sorts of mornings are interesting, don't you think? But I am glad it is sunny today. It's easier to be cheerful and cope with sadness and tragedy, when the sun is shining."

"For pity's sake," interrupted Marilla. "I've never known a girl talk so much!"

Anne could be as silent as she could be

talkative. She kept quiet at last.

The silence made Marilla feel rather uneasy. Neither she nor Matthew could think of anything to say. So the whole meal was silent.

Afterwards, Marilla asked Anne if she could wash dishes. "Pretty well," answered Anne, "but I'm better at looking after children. It's such a pity you don't have some children for me to look after."

"Just do the dishes," said Marilla, rather sharply, "and I'll think what's best to do with you."

After she had done the dishes, Anne opened the front door and was about to rush out into the sunshine. But she suddenly stopped.

"I can't go out," she sighed. "If I go out there I'll fall in love with Green Gables, the brook, the wood, everything out there. There's no point in falling in love with things if you're going be torn away from them soon after, is there?"

Marilla hurried off to the cellar to collect some stores. As she went, she started talking to herself.

"Never in all my life have I met a girl like Anne," she muttered. "Yet, as Matthew says, she is kind of interesting. I wonder what on

"Just do the dishes."

earth she'll say next. And she's cast a spell over
Matthew. She'll be casting another over me
soon."

Chapter 6
Anne's Story

On that first morning, Marilla took Anne for a ride in the horse and buggy.

"Now Anne, just you keep quiet while I think," she said, more in hope than anything else, as they set off down the track.

Anne did stay silent for a few moments. But the beauty of the day was just too much for her.

"I've made up my mind that I am going to enjoy this ride, whatever decision you come to about my future," she said. "I'm not going to think about going back to the orphanage while I'm enjoying the ride."

Marilla shook her head in disbelief as she heard Anne take a great lungful of the morning air and start talking again.

"Look at that wild pink rose," said Anne, pointing to the side of the track. "Isn't it lovely? Don't you think it would be nice to be a rose? Wouldn't it be nice if roses could talk? I'm sure they would tell us such lovely things.

"And isn't pink the most bewitching color in the world? I can't wear pink. It doesn't suit redheads like me, not even in the imagination. And by the way, are we going past the Lake of Shining Waters today?"

"No, we're not going by Barry's pond, if that's what you mean by the Lake of Shining Waters," said Marilla, glad to get a word in. "We're going by the coast road. And while you're so full of talk, why don't you tell me

Enjoying the ride

about yourself. And I don't want dreams and imaginings . . . just facts."

Anne didn't need asking twice.

"I was 11 years old last March. My mother and father were Walter and Bertha. They were high school teachers. I was told that when I was born, my mother thought I was perfectly beautiful. I'm glad she was satisfied with me. I would feel so sad if I'd been a disappointment to her, because she didn't live long after that. She died of a fever when I was three months old. Father died of the same fever a few days later."

"That left me an orphan. Folks were at their wits' end, wondering what to do with me. Eventually I was taken in by a Mrs. Thomas, who had a drunken husband. I stayed with them until I was eight. I looked after their children, but then Mr. Thomas fell under a train and died.

"Then the Hammonds took me in. I looked after their children too. Mrs. Hammond had eight babies, and three sets of twins among them. I told Mrs. Hammond that three sets were far too many. I used to get terribly tired looking after them all. Then she died too and I was sent to the orphanage."

"Did you ever go to school?" asked Marilla.

"Not really. But I read a lot at the orphanage. I know a lot of poetry too. Don't you love poetry? It gives you a crinkly, tingling feeling up and down your back."

Marilla didn't ask any more questions. She was thinking very deeply. Pity had started to stir in her heart for the little girl beside her. What a starved, unloved life Anne had led.

What if she followed Matthew's wishes and kept her? He seemed set on it and the girl did seem a nice little thing, even if she did have too much to say.

Just then, the horse and buggy turned a corner. Suddenly, below them was the sea, a shimmering blue beneath the sun. Gulls soared above the high cliffs and sandy coves.

"Isn't the sea wonderful!" exclaimed Anne. "I only ever went to the sea once. And I've lived that day in my mind ever since. Aren't the gulls nice? Would you like to be a gull? Wouldn't it be nice to wake up at dawn and swoop over the sea all day and then fly back to one's nest at sunset? I can just imagine myself doing that.

"When I get back to the orphanage, I'll imagine I am a gull and soar across the sea in my mind every day."

"Isn't the sea wonderful!"

Marilla sighed impatiently. But there was the hint of a smile on her lips.

Anne saw it. An expression of hope crossed her face.

Chapter 7
Decision Day

That evening, when Anne had gone to bed, Marilla and Matthew talked about what to do.

Hours passed and it was almost midnight when Marilla finally turned to Matthew and gave her decision.

"I've never brought up a child, let alone a girl," she began, "but after what Anne told me about her life today, I felt sorry for her. I felt as though it might be our duty to help her. I've never had anything to do with children. No doubt I'll make a mess of bringing her up, but I can only do my best. So, Matthew, as far as I am concerned, Anne can stay."

Matthew's face glowed with delight. "I thought you'd come to see it that way," he said. "She's such an interesting little thing."

"It'd be more to the point if you said she could be a useful little thing. But that's my business. I'll train her to help us. And Matthew, you're not to go interfering with my methods.

I may be an old maid who doesn't know much about bringing up a child, but I guess I know more than an old bachelor like you."

Matthew smiled. "You can have your own way, sister. Only be as good and kind to her as you can, without spoiling her. I'm sure she's one of those girls who'll do anything for you, as long as you get her to love you."

Marilla shook her head. She had little faith in Matthew understanding anything about girls.

"Now," she said firmly, "I'll bet she is still awake imagining things upstairs. But I won't tell her what we've decided until tomorrow. Otherwise she'll be so excited that she won't sleep a wink. In fact, she'd probably keep us up all night, talking!"

It was late, so Matthew decided to turn in for the night. But Marilla stayed downstairs for a little longer. She sat alone in front of the fire, thinking.

"Well, Marilla Cuthbert," she whispered to herself, "did you ever imagine the day when you would adopt a little girl? Goodness knows what will come of it. But none of us can get through this world without our share of trouble. I'll just have to make the best of it."

Decision Day

Marilla makes her decision

At last, Marilla climbed the stairs. She was about to open the door to her room when she heard Anne's voice. She tiptoed across the landing to Anne's open door and looked inside.

Anne was kneeling beside her bed in prayer.

"Dear Heavenly Father," she said, very quietly, "I thank you for the Lake of Shining Waters, the beautiful sea, the gulls, the woods, the flowers, the beautiful brook and Matthew and Marilla. That's all the blessings I can think of to thank you for, for now. As for the things I want, they're so numerous that it would take ages to name them all, so I will name just two.

"Please let me stay at Green Gables. And please let me be good-looking when I grow up."

Marilla saw Anne get back into bed, snuggle down, lay her head on the pillow and fall asleep almost immediately. She waited for a few moments and then crept across and tucked Anne up in bed. "Goodnight child," she said softly.

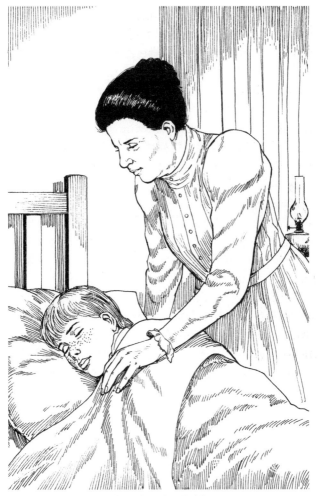

"Goodnight child."

Chapter 8
Anne of Green Gables

At breakfast, Anne was more anxious than ever to learn her fate.

"Please, oh please," she said after helping Marilla to wash the breakfast dishes, "won't you tell me if I can stay? I can't bear not knowing any more."

"Anne," answered Marilla, "stop asking me questions. Now go and hang that drying cloth outside."

Anne raced outside with the cloth and was back in an instant. She sat down at the kitchen table, looking at Marilla with big, worried eyes.

Marilla could not remain silent any more. "Anne," she said, "I suppose I might as well tell you now. Matthew and I have decided to keep you . . . that is, if you try to be a good little girl and work hard."

Marilla stopped speaking and looked at Anne, who didn't say a word. There were tears

"Matthew and I have decided to keep you."

in the girl's eyes. "Whatever is the matter child?" she asked.

"I'm crying," sniffed Anne, "but I don't know why. I'm as glad as can be. But glad isn't a big enough word for this. I was glad about the Lake of Shining Waters, the brook and the woods. But this! To stay at Green Gables . . . oh! I couldn't be happier. But . . . but . . . can you tell me why I'm crying?"

"You're overexcited, I expect," said Marilla, in a stern voice. "Try and calm yourself. I'm afraid you both cry and laugh far too easily."

Anne stopped crying. "What shall I call you, now that I am staying?" she asked. "Miss Cuthbert? Aunt Marilla?"

"Just call me Marilla. You'd make me nervous by calling me Aunt Marilla," was the reply.

"I've never had an aunt," said Anne. "I'd love to call you aunt."

"I'm not your aunt and I don't believe in calling people names that don't belong to them," said Marilla, with a shake of her head.

"Couldn't I imagine you are my aunt?"

"You couldn't," sighed Marilla. "I don't believe in imagining things. Now Anne, one thing you must learn is that when I say something, it's not an excuse to discuss it endlessly.

I shall be Marilla, and that's that! Now go outside and play."

"I shall go outside and play!" cried a happy Anne. "I shall imagine I'm a bumblebee dancing among the apple blossom. I think if I wasn't a human girl, I'd like to be a bee living among the flowers. But then it might be nice to be an apple tree dressed in all that blossom. But if I was an apple tree I wouldn't want a bee to come stealing all my blossom . . ."

Marilla despaired of the girl. "Now Anne, remember this," she said, in a firm voice. "You are not a bumblebee, nor an apple tree."

"I know I'm not really," said Anne, dancing up to a mirror on the wall.

She looked at herself in the mirror for a moment and then spoke. "No, I am just Anne of Green Gables now, and I think it's a million times better to be Anne of Green Gables than anyone or anything else in the world."

Anne of Green Gables

Chapter 9
Rachel's Visit

Marilla's neighbor Rachel lived in a house beside the brook, below Green Gables. Nothing moved in Avonlea without her knowing it.

Rachel sat by her kitchen window, knitting from dawn to dusk. She missed no one coming or going. Not even the brook could run past her house without being inspected by Rachel. The woman loved to gossip.

She was the first to learn that Marilla and Matthew were adopting an orphan. She was also the first to hear that the child was a girl orphan, rather than the boy everyone was expecting.

So it was not surprising that Rachel was the first to inspect the new arrival.

Marilla met her at the front door of Green Gables. "I've come to see the orphan," said Rachel, without so much as a "Good evening".

"I'm just getting over the surprise of it all," answered Marilla.

"It's too bad the child is a girl," said Rachel. "Couldn't you send her back?"

"We could, I suppose. But Matthew took a fancy to her. And I must say that I like her too. She has her faults. But she's a really bright little thing."

"There's no guessing how a girl like that might turn out," said Rachel seriously. "But I don't want to put you off the idea."

"You won't put me off the idea," said Marilla firmly. "When I make up my mind to do something, it stays made up."

Just then Anne came running in, her face sparkling with happiness and delight.

Rachel took one look at Anne's red hair and freckles and her skinny little body.

"My, my!" she chirped. "Look at those freckles and red hair. And those skinny little legs. She's a bit ugly, isn't she. You certainly didn't choose her for her good looks, did you Marilla. Come here child. Come closer!"

Anne did go closer, but not exactly as Rachel had expected.

With one bound she crossed the kitchen and stood before Rachel. Her face was scarlet with anger, her lips quivering and her whole slender body trembling from head to foot.

"I've come to see the orphan."

"I hate you!" she yelled, her voice almost choking and her feet stamping the ground. "I hate you! I hate you! How dare you call me skinny and ugly? How dare you say I'm freckly and redheaded? You are a rude, unkind woman!"

"Anne!" cried Marilla, in shock.

But Anne wasn't finished. "How dare you say such things about me? How would you like to be told you are fat and clumsy, or that you haven't got an ounce of imagination? And

"I hate you!"

I don't care if I have hurt your feelings, because you have hurt mine worse than they've ever been hurt before. And I'll never forgive you! Never! Never!"

Rachel was horrified. "Did anyone see such a temper?" she shrieked.

"Go to your room, Anne," said Marilla. "Right now!"

Anne burst into tears, ran out of the room and leapt up the stairs like a whirlwind.

Chapter 10
Anne's Punishment

"Well, I don't envy your job in bringing up *that* one," snapped Rachel, as she heard Anne's bedroom door slam shut like a crash of thunder.

Marilla opened her mouth, but she wasn't sure what she wanted to say. The words that did come out surprised her then and forever afterwards.

"Rachel, can you blame the girl?" she said. "You shouldn't have teased her about her looks."

Rachel went red in the face. "Are you telling me, Marilla Cuthbert," she said, "that you support the girl and her terrible display of temper?"

"No," said Marilla slowly. "I can't excuse her temper. She has been very naughty and I will have to speak to her about her behavior. But perhaps we should make some allowances for her. She's never been taught what is right and wrong. No one's ever loved her. And you *were* very hard on her."

Rachel moved toward the kitchen door, as if to leave. "Well, if that's how you see it," she gasped, "then I'll have to watch my words. But I never thought I'd see the day when an ugly orphan girl's feelings had to be considered before mine."

Rachel took a deep breath and continued. "Take this advice from someone who has brought up ten children and buried two. Take a birch stick to her. She'll understand that language. Her hair matches her temper for sure. Now, good evening Marilla, and don't expect me to come a-visiting here again in a hurry."

Rachel swept through the door and left.

Marilla closed the door and hurried upstairs to Anne's bedroom. She wasn't sure what to do, although she knew she wouldn't take Rachel's advice and whip her with a birch stick.

Marilla found Anne face-down on her bed. She was crying loudly.

"Anne!" she said impatiently. "Get off that bed this minute and listen to what I have to say."

Anne slowly got off the bed and sat down on a chair beside it. Her face was swollen and tear-stained. Her eyes were fixed stubbornly on the floor.

"Aren't you ashamed of yourself, Anne?" Marilla asked.

"She had no right to call me ugly and red-headed," replied Anne defiantly.

"And you had no right to lose your temper with Rachel," said Marilla. "I was ashamed of you. You disgraced me. You are a naughty little girl."

Anne bit her lip. "You'd find it easier," she said, "to be bad rather than good if you had red hair. It's not easy having red hair."

"I don't understand why you should have got so angry at what Rachel said," continued Marilla. "You yourself say you are red-headed and ugly some times."

"Oh, but there's such a big difference in between saying a thing yourself and hearing other people say it," wailed Anne. "You may know a thing, but you can't help hoping that other people don't quite think it."

"Never mind," said Marilla. "You've made a fine exhibition of yourself and Rachel will have a nice story to gossip about. And she will be sure to tell everyone, too."

"Just imagine how you would have felt," pleaded Anne tearfully "if someone told you to your face that you were skinny and ugly."

Anne's Punishment

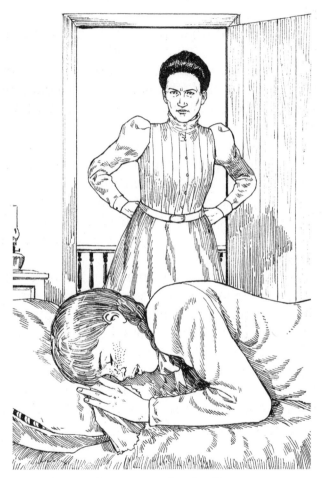

Anne was crying loudly.

Suddenly, an old memory flitted into Marilla's mind. She recalled how hurt she had been as a child when an old aunt told her she was ugly.

Her words softened after that.

"I didn't say that Rachel was right to say what she did," she said, "but equally, there was no excuse for what you said to her. You must go and tell her you are sorry. Ask her to forgive you."

Anne looked more defiant than ever. "I can never do that. You can punish me in any way you want. You can shut me up in a dark, damp dungeon. You can feed me bread and water and I'll not complain. But I cannot ask Rachel to forgive me."

Marilla felt the beginnings of a smile creeping onto her face at the thought of what Anne had just said. "We're not in the habit of putting little girls in dungeons around here," she said. "But apologize to Rachel you must and shall. And you'll stay in your room until you do."

"I shall have to stay here forever then," said Anne sadly. "How can I tell Rachel I'm sorry, when I'm not sorry? I'm sorry I disappointed you. I'm sorry I made you angry with me. But I'm glad I told her what I did. It gave me great satisfaction. I can't even *imagine* I'm sorry."

Anne's Punishment

Refusing to apologize

"Perhaps your imagination will be working better in the morning," said Marilla. "You can have the night to think it over."

Marilla went downstairs to the kitchen. And there she sat down in a chair. Suddenly, the image of Rachel's red and angry face came into her mind.

Marilla's lips twitched in amusement at the thought of it. She felt an almost uncontrollable urge to laugh.

Chapter 11
The Apology

There was no apology from Anne the next morning. Stubbornly, she remained in her bedroom.

At breakfast, Marilla told her brother what had happened between Anne and Rachel.

"Rachel is a meddlesome old gossip!" said Matthew. "I'm sorry I missed hearing Anne tell her off."

"Matthew Cuthbert!" said an astonished Marilla. "You know that Anne's behavior was dreadful. I suppose you'll be saying next she shouldn't be punished at all."

"Well, no, not exactly," said Matthew. "Perhaps she should be punished a little. But don't be too hard on her and make sure you give her something to eat for breakfast."

"Of course I will," snapped Marilla. "Anne will have her meals, but she'll have to stay in her room until she's ready to apologize to Rachel. And that's final."

Marilla did take Anne her breakfast. But the girl was neither eating nor apologizing.

Later, when Marilla was outside milking the cows, Matthew sneaked into Anne's room.

"How are you?" he whispered, fearing Marilla would suddenly come upstairs and surprise him.

"Pretty well," she smiled, bravely facing the thought that she might have to spend many long years alone in her room.

"Come on Anne," begged Matthew, "why don't you apologize? Marilla's a dreadfully determined woman. And busybody Rachel is not worth the trouble."

Anne thought for a moment. "I suppose I could apologize to oblige you," she said at last. "Do you really want me to?"

"Of course I do. It terribly lonesome downstairs without you."

"Very well," announced Anne, "I'll tell Marilla that I've given in. I will apologize to Rachel."

Matthew whispered something even more quietly. "Don't tell Marilla I had anything to do with it."

"Wild horses wouldn't drag the secret out of me," laughed Anne. "Not that I understand

"Why don't you apologize?"

how a wild horse could drag anything out of a person."

*

Later that evening, Marilla took Anne over to Rachel's house to apologize."

"Oh, Rachel, I am extremely sorry," Anne began, in the most humble way she could imagine. "I could never express all my sorrow for what I did, not if I used up the whole dictionary. I have behaved terribly to you and embarrassed my dear friends, Matthew and Marilla, who let me stay at Green Gables even though I'm not a boy. I deserve to be punished and cast out into the woods for what I've done."

Marilla raised her eyes to the ceiling as Anne rambled on. Rachel looked bemused.

"It was a wicked thing for me to fly into a temper just because you told me the truth," continued Anne. "Every word was true. My hair is red. I'm freckled, skinny and ugly. Oh Rachel, please forgive me for what I said."

Anne clasped her hands together, bowed her head and waited for Rachel's decision.

"You're forgiven, child," said Rachel, shaking her head in confusion. "I guess I was a

The Apology

"I have behaved terribly to you."

little too hard on you. Besides, I knew a girl your age with red hair and it turned into a beautiful auburn by the time she grew up."

"Oh, you've given me hope," cried Anne, running towards the door. "I must hurry and tell the apple trees that I might grow into a beautiful child even yet."

"She really is a strange little thing," said Rachel, after Anne had gone outside. "But I can see something of why you wanted to keep her."

The early evening stars were in the sky by the time Marilla and Anne set off to walk back to Green Gables.

"I apologized pretty well, didn't I?" said Anne. "If you've got to apologize, you might as well make a proper job of it."

Once more, Marilla felt a smile coming on.

Anne didn't see it. She was already away in some imaginary world. "Aren't the stars bright tonight," she said. "If you could live in a star, which one would you pick?"

"Do ever stop imagining things?" asked Marilla.

"Sometimes," answered Anne, her eyes dreamily searching the horizon.

But the next light she saw was the cheerful

gleam coming from the kitchen window at Green Gables.

Anne suddenly moved closer to Marilla and slipped a hand into hers.

"It's lovely to be going home and know it's home," she said. "I have never loved any place before. But I love Green Gables already."

Something warm and pleasant welled up in Marilla's heart, as she felt that thin little hand squeeze hers.

"Do you know," said Anne, "tonight I'm going to imagine that I'm the wind blowing through the trees. I'll fly over Rachel's house and set the flowers dancing. And I'll sail across the Lake of Shining Waters and ripple it all up into little sparkling waves. Oh, there's so much room for imagination in a wind! But for now, I'll not talk any more. I'll just look at the stars."

"Oh, thank goodness for that," thought Marilla, happy to hear the little girl fall silent at last.

Chapter 12
A New Friend

The next day, Marilla announced that she knew a little girl who might become Anne's first friend.

"It's Diana Barry," she said, "and she's about your age. Her father owns that pond you call the Lake of Shining Waters."

The Barry family lived on the opposite side of the valley. Marilla drove Anne over in the gig that afternoon. Mrs. Barry answered the door. She had a reputation for being very strict with her children.

"So this is the girl you have adopted," said Mrs. Barry.

"Yes, this is Anne," replied Marilla.

"Anne, spelled with an *e*," added Anne, making sure the woman understood that she wasn't any ordinary Ann.

Mrs. Barry raised an eyebrow. "Never mind how you spell your name," she said. "I'll go and find Diana."

A New Friend

Diana was a very pretty girl, with her mother's dark hair and dark eyes, and rosy cheeks.

"You two can go and play in the garden," said Mrs. Barry.

It was a beautiful garden full of blooming flowers and shrubs.

For a moment or two the two girls were silent, slightly shy of what to say to each other. But then Anne asked a question. "Do you think you could like me – have me as a friend?"

Diana laughed. She always laughed before she spoke. "Of course! I'm so glad you've come to live at Green Gables. It will be lovely to have someone of my own age to play with. I've only got a sister called Minnie and she's still a baby."

That afternoon, they ran hand-in-hand through the garden and played all sorts of games.

"Will you swear to be my friend for ever and ever?" Anne asked.

"Of course I will," answered Diana. "And will you come and see me tomorrow?"

Anne promised she would. "And we'll go and build a playhouse in the woods."

That evening, Marilla asked how she had got on with Diana.

"We'll be friends forever," said Anne. "I'm going to see her again tomorrow."

"Don't forget you've got jobs around the house to finish before you can go and play," said Marilla. "And will you make me a promise before you go?"

"Yes," said Anne, a little puzzled.

"Please don't talk Diana to death," said Marilla quietly.

*

Anne was very excited when she returned from playing with Diana the next day.

"There's going to be a picnic by the Lake of Shining Waters on Monday afternoon," she said. "There'll be cake and sandwiches, and Rachel is going to make some ice cream, too. Think of it, Marilla, ice cream! Oh, Marilla, can I go to it?"

"I don't see why not," said Marilla.

"I've never been to a picnic. I've often dreamed of going to one. Diana says that everyone must take a basket of things to eat. But I can't cook. I'd feel terribly embarrassed if I had to go without a basket."

Marilla told Anne not to worry. She would

A New Friend

Playing in the garden

bake some pies and bread to take.

Anne leapt at Marilla and planted a great kiss on her cheek. Marilla had never felt such affection, but she still wasn't quite able to show Anne how the kiss had warmed her heart.

Asking to go to the picnic

Chapter 13
The Missing Locket

Anne hardly slept for the next few days. She was starting to imagine the picnic. Would Monday ever come?

"You set your heart on things too much," Marilla said to Anne. "I'm afraid there will be disappointments in your life sometimes."

"Oh Marilla," smiled Anne, "half the pleasure of things is looking forward to them. If they don't happen, you can still remember the fun you had looking forward to them."

Anne didn't know it then, but a disappointment was waiting to happen just the next day, which was Sunday.

Marilla had a favorite locket on a chain that she wore to church every Sunday. Anne always loved to see her wear it.

Marilla told Anne that the locket was her most treasured possession. A seafaring uncle had given it to her. It was made of silver and had a purple-colored amethyst stone set into it. Inside it was a lock of Marilla's mother's hair.

But that Sunday morning the locket was nowhere to be found.

"Have you seen my locket?" Marilla asked Anne, when she came into the kitchen for Sunday breakfast.

"I saw it Friday morning," answered Anne, "when you were outside bringing in the cows for milking. I was passing your bedroom and saw it on the table beside your bed."

Marilla asked whether Anne had touched it.

"Yes," admitted Anne. "I picked it up and pinned it on my dress, to see what it would look like."

Marilla was angry. "You had no business to do that, or go into my room in the first place. Where is the locket now?"

"I put it back on the table," answered Anne innocently. "I only had it on for a few seconds. I didn't mean to meddle."

"You can't have put it back," said Marilla. "The locket isn't anywhere to be seen. You must have taken it out."

"I did put it back," insisted Anne. "I'm certain of that. I never took the locket out of your room. So there!"

The Missing Locket

Pinning the locket on her dress

Anne's **so there** was only her way of making her point. But Marilla mistook it for defiance.

"I think you are lying, Anne," she said. "Go to your room until you're ready to tell the truth."

Anne went back to her bedroom without another word.

Marilla was very upset. She was sure Anne wouldn't have stolen it, but she might have lost it and been frightened to tell the truth.

She told Matthew about it later that day. He was sure that Anne would never have taken the locket. "Perhaps it's fallen down behind the bedroom table," he suggested.

"I've looked there, and in every nook and cranny," snapped Marilla. "No, the child must have taken it and lied to me. That's the plain, ugly truth Matthew Cuthbert. She must stay in her room until she confesses!"

A little later Marilla went up to see Anne. She had been crying. "It's no good you crying," said Marilla sharply. "Just tell me what you've done with the locket. You'll stay here until you do!"

"But it's the picnic tomorrow," wailed Anne. "I must go to it."

"You're not going anywhere until you've confessed," said Marilla.

The next morning, Marilla brought some breakfast up to Anne's room. She found the girl sitting upright in bed. "I'm ready to confess," Anne announced.

Marilla was quite shocked to hear the words.

"Yes, I confess," repeated Anne. "I took the locket, just as you said. It was so beautiful that I was overcome by temptation. I imagined how wonderful it would be to take it to show Diana and pretend I was Lady Cordelia Fitzgerald. So I did.

"I thought I could put the locket back before you came home. But I stopped on the little bridge and took it out, to look at it in the sunlight. And that's when I dropped it into the river. The locket sank without trace. And that's the best I can do at confessing, Marilla."

Marilla lost her temper. "You are the wickedest girl I ever met."

"Yes, I suppose I am," said Anne quietly. "And I know I have to be punished. Please punish me now so that I don't have to worry about it when I go to the picnic."

"Picnic indeed!" exploded Marilla. "You'll go to no picnic today, Anne! That will be your punishment. And it isn't anywhere big enough a punishment for what you've done!"

"I'm ready to confess."

Chapter 14
The Mystery Solved

"Not go to the picnic!" shouted Anne, spring-
ing to her feet. "But you said if I confessed . . .
oh Marilla, I must go to the picnic! That was
why I confessed. Punish me in any way you like
but let me go to the picnic."

Anne clutched Marilla's hands. "Think of the
ice cream. I may never have a chance of tasting
ice cream ever again."

"It's my final word," said Marilla. "You are
not going."

Anne gave a piercing shriek and threw
herself face-down on the bed.

Marilla went downstairs thinking that
perhaps she should have followed Rachel's
advice and sent the child straight back to the
orphanage.

Later, Marilla called Anne for lunch. She
appeared at the top of the stairs. "I don't want
any lunch," she sobbed. "I couldn't eat anything. My heart is broken. You broke it,

Marilla. But I forgive you. Remember that I forgive you. But please don't ask me to eat anything, especially boiled pork and greens. Boiled pork and greens are so unromantic when one is suffering so much sadness."

Marilla left Anne where she was and went to have lunch with Matthew. It was a dismal meal. Neither spoke a word.

Afterwards, Marilla went upstairs to mend a small rip in a shawl she had worn on the previous Friday. She had left the shawl in her mending box.

Now, as she picked it out of the box, the sun sparkled on something. Marilla looked closer. It was the locket, hanging by a thread from the shawl.

"My goodness!" exclaimed Marilla. "What on earth does this mean? Here's my locket safe and sound, when I thought it was at the bottom of the river."

Marilla scratched her head for a moment. "I remember now," she thought. "I took my shawl off on the Friday and I must have laid it on the bedroom table for a moment before putting it in the mending box. That's when the locket must have got caught up in it. Why did Anne say she took it and lost it? She couldn't have!"

"I don't want any lunch."

Marilla hurried to Anne's bedroom. The girl was still lying face-down on her bed. "Anne Shirley," she said solemnly, "I've just found my locket hanging to my shawl. Now, I want to know what all that nonsense about dropping it in the river was about."

Anne began slowly. "You said you'd keep me here until I confessed. So I decided to confess, because I was so desperate to go the picnic. I thought out my confession and made it sound as interesting as I could. But then you wouldn't let me go to the picnic anyway, so all the trouble I went to was wasted."

Marilla could have laughed, but she realized that Anne was still very upset at not going to the picnic.

"Anne," she said, "you beat everything. I should never have doubted what you said. It wasn't right to confess to something you hadn't done. But I must have driven you to it. Please forgive me, Anne. And now get yourself ready for the picnic."

Anne leapt from the bed. "Do you mean it isn't too late?" she screamed in delight.

"It's only two o'clock," said Marilla. "Most of the people won't even have got there yet."

Anne washed and dressed, while Marilla

went and filled a basket with food.

Soon she came flying down the stairs. "Five minutes ago I was so miserable and wished I hadn't been born," she cried. "And now I wouldn't change places with an angel!"

*

Anne returned exhausted to Green Gables that night. "I've had a perfectly scrumptious time," she said. "Scrumptious is a new word I learned today. I heard Jane Andrews use it. Everything was lovely. We went rowing on the Lake of Shining Waters. Jane Andrews nearly fell overboard. And we all had ice cream. Words fail me. Marilla, it was absolutely . . . sublime!"

Later, Marilla told the whole story to Matthew. "Do you know something," she said, "that child is hard to understand sometimes, but she'll turn out all right yet. One thing's for sure . . . no house will ever be dull with her inside it."

And how Marilla and Matthew were agreed on that!

She came flying down the stairs.

Chapter 15
Off to School

The day soon arrived when Anne started at Avonlea School.

"What a splendid morning!" said Anne, as she set off with her friend Diana, in the sunshine. "Isn't it good just to be alive on a day like this? I pity the people who aren't born yet for missing it."

Anne and Diana walked hand-in-hand to the school – a low wooden whitewashed building.

Inside was a single room full of old-fashioned wooden desks, with tops that opened and shut. Most of the desks were carved with the names of children who had been at Avonlea School long ago.

The teacher's name was Mr. Phillips. Anne didn't like him very much. He was a stern man, who never seemed to smile.

The first day was full of excitement for Anne and before she knew it, it was over.

When she got home that evening, she announced that she was probably going to enjoy school.

"I sat next to Diana at a desk by the window. We can see the Lake of Shining Waters from there. There are a lot of nice girls at the school. Ruby Gillis gave me an apple. Sophia Sloane wanted to walk me home. Tillie Boulter let me wear her beads all afternoon. And Jane Andrews told me that Minnie MacPherson thought I had a pretty nose. But Diana will always be my best friend."

Anne said there was one problem. Because of her early years in the orphanage, the other children were all ahead of her in most subjects.

But Anne did come top in one subject. "No one can match me for imagination!" she cried proudly.

*

Of course, there were also boys at Avonlea School. Sophia Sloane's brother Charlie took a liking to Anne.

"Charlie reckons you're the smartest girl in school," Diana told Anne, one day. "And being

Off to School

First day at Avonlea School

the smartest is even better than being the prettiest."

"No it isn't," replied Anne. "I'd rather be pretty than clever. In any case, I hate Charlie Sloane. I can't bear a boy with goggle eyes."

There was another boy called Gilbert Blythe in Anne's class. "Don't you think he's handsome?" asked Diana.

Anne looked across at the classroom and saw that Gilbert had just pinned Ruby Gillis' long golden braid to the back of her chair.

Moments later she went to move forward and almost pulled her hair out at the roots. In the chaos that followed, Gilbert pulled out the pin and sat back as though he had done absolutely nothing. He was so cheeky, he even winked at Anne.

"Yes, he's handsome," said Anne later, "but he's a bit bold. Is it good manners to wink at a strange girl?"

In the afternoon, Gilbert leaned over and caught Anne by her hair. Before she could free herself, he had whispered one word: "Carrots!"

Anne jumped to her feet, her red hair flying in the air. Then, thwack! She cracked Gilbert across the head with her geography book.

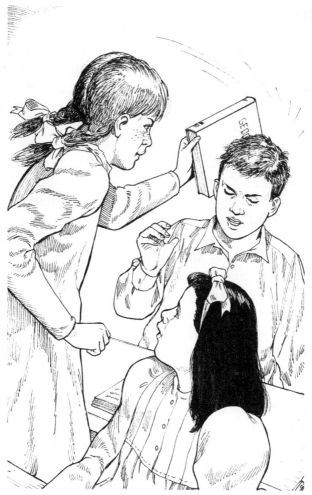

Then, thwack!

Avonlea School always enjoyed a scene. Diana gasped. Ruby Gillis became hysterical. Charlie Sloane roared with laughter.

Mr. Phillips walked over to Anne, looking very stern. "And what's going on here?" he demanded to know.

Anne did not say a word. She didn't want the whole school to know that she was upset at being called carrots, because of the color of her hair.

But Gilbert did speak. "It was my fault," he confessed. "I teased her."

Mr. Phillips would not listen. "I don't like my pupils showing such a temper. Anne, go and stand in front of the blackboard for the rest of the afternoon.

As soon as she was standing in front of the blackboard, Mr. Phillips took a piece of chalk and wrote on the blackboard above her head:

Ann Shirley has a very bad temper. Ann Shirley must learn to control her temper

Anne might not have been so angry if Mr. Phillips had spelt her name correctly, with an *e* at the end!

Chapter 16
A Sworn Enemy

Gilbert Blythe tried to talk to Anne when she and Diana arrived at school the next morning.

"I'm really sorry I made fun of your hair, Anne," he said. "Please don't be mad at me."

Anne swept past him without even turning her head.

"How could you ignore him like that?" asked Diana. "Most of the other girls would die to be even noticed by Gilbert Blythe."

"I shall never forgive him for calling me names and getting me into trouble," announced Anne.

Diana told her not to take any notice of what Gilbert had said. "He makes fun of lots of the girls. He laughs at my hair because it is so dark. He says I look like a crow."

Anne reckoned there a great deal of difference between being called a crow and being called carrots.

"Gilbert Blythe has hurt my feelings," she said angrily.

The next day there was more trouble. Some of the children were late for school. Anne was on time, but Mr. Phillips made a mistake and also punished her for being late.

Anne's punishment was to be moved from the desk beside Diana to the one next to Gilbert.

To Anne, this seemed so unfair. Firstly, she had been wrongly punished. And secondly, she had been forced to sit beside Gilbert – a boy who had insulted her. She felt utterly humiliated and put her head down on her desk, unable to work. Gilbert tried to speak to her again, but she continued to ignore him.

When school ended that day, she told Diana that she would not be coming back again.

Diana could not believe what Anne had said. "Marilla will never let you stay at home," she said.

"She'll have to!" insisted Anne, crossing her arms and looking defiant. "I'll never go to school with Mr. Phillips there ever again."

She said the same to Marilla when she got home.

"Nonsense," said Marilla, "you've got to go to school."

A Sworn Enemy

"Please don't be mad at me."

"I've been insulted and treated unfairly," cried Anne. "I shall learn my lessons at home."

Marilla saw the stubbornness in Anne's eyes and decided there was no point in reasoning with her just then. Instead, she went to get advice from Rachel.

"Of course, Mr. Phillips was both right and wrong," Rachel said to Marilla. "He did right to punish her for losing her temper with Gilbert but he did wrong to punish her for being late when she wasn't. Let her stay at home for a while. She'll soon cool off and want to go back to her friends at school. They all like her at school, you know."

So that's what Marilla did.

Anne stayed at home and did her lessons, as well as her chores around the house. Diana came to play with her too.

One day Anne passed Gilbert on the road. She gave him an icy look and walked on by without saying a word.

Diana tried to make peace between the two, but it seemed that Anne had made up her mind to ignore Gilbert for the rest of her life.

A Sworn Enemy

"I shall learn my lessons at home."

Chapter 17
The Disastrous Tea Party

Anne's fondness for Diana grew and grew. They spent all their spare time together. One day, Anne decided to organize a tea party for her friend.

"Can I use the best china teapot and cups?" she asked Marilla.

"Of course not," said Marilla. "I only use those for important callers. You'll have to use the old brown teapot and tea set. But you can have some of my fruit cake and cookies."

"I can just imagine myself sitting at the head of the table and pouring tea," said Anne excitedly. "Of course, I shall ask Diana if she takes sugar. I know she doesn't, but I can ask her just as if I didn't know."

"There's a bottle of fresh raspberry juice you can offer her too," said Marilla. "It's on the second shelf in the kitchen cupboard."

"Oh, it's going to be such fun," cried Anne.

The Disastrous Tea Party

Diana arrived for tea and was met at the door by Anne.

The two play-acted for a while, as if they grown-ups. They shook hands and made small talk about the weather and their families.

"And how is your family?" asked Anne, so politely.

"Oh, very well," replied Diana. "And yours?"

"Very well, indeed," said Anne.

But it wasn't long before they began to eat their tea. First they had tomato sandwiches that Marilla had made. Then they gobbled up the fruitcake and cookies.

To finish, Anne went to the kitchen cupboard and took down the bottle of raspberry juice from the second shelf.

She poured a glass of the juice for Diana and gave it to her. "I'm too full to have anything else," said Anne, "but you can have as much juice as you want."

Diana swallowed her juice very quickly. "This is delicious," she said. "It's the nicest I've ever tasted."

Anne poured her a second glass, and a third.

It was when Diana had finished the third that she started to feel rather ill.

She poured a glass of the juice for Diana.

She stood up unsteadily and put her hands to her head. Then she sat down again. "Oh, I feel sick," she moaned. "I feel dizzy and funny all over. I must go home."

"Oh, please don't go home yet," pleaded Anne, "we haven't even had a cup of tea!"

But Diana got up again and walked towards the door. "I must go home," was all she could say.

Anne walked her most of the way home and then returned to Green Gables.

She was so unhappy that her tea party had gone badly. But nothing more was said about it until the next day, when Marilla came home after calling on Diana's mother.

"Anne!" she said. "Mrs. Barry says you made Diana drunk. What on earth did you give her?"

Anne was so shocked. "Nothing except raspberry juice," she replied. "I never thought people got drunk on raspberry juice . . . not even if they drank three big glasses like Diana did."

Marilla suddenly raised her hands to her head in horror. "Oh, Anne, you certainly have a genius for getting into trouble. I think you must have taken my currant wine instead of the raspberry juice. The wine has alcohol in it. Now

"I must go home."

that would have made her drunk. Don't you know the difference between raspberry juice and wine?"

"I've never tasted wine before," Anne said quietly. "I just thought it was raspberry juice, like you said."

"Oh dear," answered Marilla. "Mrs. Barry says she'll never let you play with Diana again."

Anne burst into tears.

"Oh, don't cry, Anne. She'll forgive you when I tell her the truth."

But when Marilla returned from seeing Mrs. Barry there was more bad news.

"What an awful woman," she sighed. "I told her it was all a mistake and you weren't to blame, but she didn't believe me. And on top of that, she said I was a wicked woman to have currant wine in the house . . . and I only use a few drops of it in winter to cure colds."

Anne didn't answer, but ran out of the house and raced over to the Barry's home. Almost out of breath, she knocked at the door.

Mrs. Barry answered it. "What do you want?" she asked, stiffly.

"Oh, Mrs. Barry, please forgive me. I really did think it was raspberry juice. Why would

I want to get Diana drunk? She is my best friend. Please don't say you won't let Diana play with me any more."

The speech might have softened the heart of any woman, except Mrs. Barry. "I don't think you are a fit girl for Diana to be friends with. You'd better go home and try and behave yourself in future," she said.

Anne's lip quivered. "Won't you let me see Diana just to say goodbye?"

"Please forgive me."

"No!" said Mrs. Barry, sharply. "Now go home!"

With that, she closed the door.

That night, Marilla tried to comfort Anne. But it was no good. The little girl cried herself to sleep.

Chapter 18
Back to School

The next afternoon, Anne looked out of the window and saw Diana waving to her from near the brook.

Anne flew out of the house and raced down to see her. "Has your mother forgiven me?" she asked breathlessly.

"No," said Diana. "She still says I'm never to play with you again. I've cried and cried. I've told her it wasn't your fault, but it wasn't any use. She did say I could come and say goodbye to you, though. She's given me ten minutes and she's timing me by the clock."

"Ten minutes isn't long to say goodbye to your best friend," sobbed Anne. "Oh, Diana, tell me you'll never forget me."

"Of course I'll never forget you. I'll never have a friend as close and dear as you. I couldn't love anybody as I love you."

Anne had never in her whole life been told

that someone loved her.

"You love me?" said Anne, surprised by what she'd heard.

"Why, of course," said Diana.

"I thought you liked me but I never thought you loved me," smiled Anne, wiping the tears from her cheeks. "I didn't think anybody could love me. Oh, this is so wonderful. It's like a ray of light in a dark tunnel.

"I always will love you, Anne," said Diana.

The two girls hugged each other and Anne asked Diana to send her a lock of her hair to keep. Diana picked up a sharp stone right then, and cut off a small length and gave it to her.

Then she was gone. Anne watched her give one last wave before disappearing into the distance.

"It's all over," Anne told Marilla, when she got home. "Mrs. Barry won't forgive me. I shall never have another friend."

"I don't think there is any fear of you not having another friend," said Marilla, "as long as you can talk like you do."

The next morning, Marilla was surprised to see Anne coming downstairs with her schoolbooks.

"I'm going back to school," she said solemnly. "It's all that's left in life for me now ... now that my dearest friend has been stolen from me. In school I can look at her and think about the great friend I once had."

"Perhaps you could also look at your books and think about learning something as well," said Marilla, hardly able to hide her joy that Anne was going back to school. "And don't go cracking anyone over the head with your books!"

"I'll try to be a model pupil," said Anne. "It won't be much fun for me. But I'll try."

*

Anne was welcomed back to school with open arms by everyone. Her imagination had been sorely missed in every class.

Ruby Gillis brought her three plums for a present. Jane Andrews and Minnie Macpherson brought her flowers. Sophia Sloane gave her some new sewing needles. Katie Boulter gave her some perfume and Julia Bell wrote a poem for her.

On her desk was a small parcel from Diana, with a letter stuck to the top of it.

Then she was gone.

Anne read the letter.

Dear Anne,
Mother says I'm not to play with you or talk to you, even in school. Don't be cross at me. I love you as much as ever. I miss you awfully. I've made you one of my bookmarks out of red tissue paper. They are very fashionable now and only three girls in school know how to make them. So remember me when you look at it.
Your true friend,
Diana

Anne kissed the bookmark and then wrote a short reply on a page from her schoolbook.

Dear Diana,
Of course I am not cross with you. You have to obey your mother. We'll have to let our spirits talk to each other instead. I shall keep your lovely present forever. I shall sleep with your letter under my pillow tonight.
Yours until death do us part,
Anne (or Lady Cordelia Fitzgerald)

Back to School

Being welcomed back to school

Chapter 19
Anne to the Rescue

For the next few weeks, Anne was a model pupil. She studied hard and did all her homework on time. She became very competitive and wanted to be top of the class in every subject.

Anne and Gilbert still didn't speak. Anne proved to be an expert in holding grudges. But an unspoken rivalry sprang up between them.

Anne never hinted to anyone that she was determined to beat Gilbert in class, but that was her aim. Some weeks she came top of the class in spelling and English. And other weeks, it was Gilbert.

There were also new subjects to be learned now, such as Latin, French, algebra . . . and the dreaded geometry.

Anne just couldn't understand geometry at all.

"Geometry's perfectly awful stuff," she told Marilla. "I can't make head nor tail of it. And there's definitely no room for the imagination in it. Mr. Phillips says I am a total dunce at geometry. And Gilbert gets top marks all the time. Even Diana gets along better than I do. But I don't mind being beaten by Diana."

Marilla asked if she had spoken to Diana yet.

"No," she answered, "and it makes me very sad that we don't talk."

*

A few nights later, as the first winter snow descended on Avonlea, Anne was alone with Matthew at Green Gables.

Just about everyone in Avonlea had gone to Charlottetown, the main town on Prince Edward Island, to listen to the Canadian Premier giving a speech.

Anne and Matthew were sitting in front of the fire, when they heard an urgent knock on the door. It was Diana Barry.

"Oh Anne, do come quickly!" cried Diana, ashen-faced with worry. "It's my sister, baby Minnie. She's got a terrible fever. She's so hot. Mother and Father are away in town, and there's nobody to go for the doctor."

Matthew hurried off to the stable. "I'll take the buggy and get the doctor," he shouted back. "Anne, you go with Diana and do what you can!"

The two girls ran off hand-in-hand down the snowy track, across the brook and river, and up to the Barry's place.

Minnie was only two years old, and she looked very sick as she lay in her cot in the kitchen. She was feverish and restless. At times she seemed unable to breathe properly. Anne felt her forehead.

"What is it?" cried Diana. What's wrong with her? I'm sure she'll die before my mother gets home."

"No she won't," said Anne calmly. "I'll see if I can find something in the medical cabinet to treat her."

Anne hunted through the medical cabinet in the bathroom. She found exactly what she wanted. The label on the bottle said:

Fever treatment for young children

Anne took it into the kitchen and read the instructions on the label. Then she poured a little of the contents into a cup. Gently, she

"Oh Anne, do come quickly!"

poured the mixture down the baby's throat.

An hour later she did the same, and then again the following hour. As each hour passed, Minnie seemed to get a little better. She could breathe more easily and the fever cooled.

By the time the doctor arrived, Minnie was much better and sleeping soundly.

"She was feverish and couldn't breathe," explained Anne, "so I gave her some of that fever medicine."

"My goodness," said the doctor. "How on earth did you know what to do?"

Anne explained how she had learned how to treat baby fever when she was living with Mrs. Hammond, who had three sets of twins. "I used to look after them," she said. "They all got the fever at one time or another. I saw what the doctor did then. That's why I knew what to do."

"You did everything right!" said the doctor. "You saved this little girl's life."

The doctor stayed behind with Diana while Matthew took Anne home. She was exhausted and fell asleep as soon as her head touched the pillow.

Anne slept late the next morning. She awoke when Marilla came to give her some news.

"You saved this little girl's life."

"Oh Anne, you are such a clever girl. Mrs. Barry called in, early this morning. She says you saved Minnie's life and she wants to apologize for how she treated you over the currant wine affair."

And the best news of all was that Mrs. Barry wanted Anne to be Diana's best friend forever!

Anne didn't need asking twice. She was out of bed and dressed in moments. Then she was flying across the meadow, over the brook and river, and up the hill to the Barry's house.

Anne returned to Green Gables later that day. "You see before you a perfectly happy person, now that Diana and I can be friends again," she declared. "I'm perfectly happy, in spite of my red hair!"

Chapter 20
The Concert

Late one evening, Anne came hurrying downstairs at Green Gables and told Marilla that she wanted to run over and visit Diana.

"Why ever do you want to go out in the snow at this time of night?" asked Marilla.

"Diana wants to see me," said Anne. "She's got something very important to tell me."

"How do you know that?" asked Marilla. "You haven't seen Diana since this morning."

"She signaled to me from her window," answered Anne.

Marilla was puzzled until Anne explained that the two girls had arranged a way to signal to each other with candles and bits of cardboard.

"We set the candle on the windowsill and make flashes of light by passing the cardboard up and down in front of the candle. So many flashes mean a certain thing. It was my idea."

Marilla was amazed. "You'll be setting the

curtains on fire next with your signaling nonsense," she said.

"We're very careful and it's fun," replied Anne.

She explained that one flash meant "Are you there?" Two meant "Yes". It was three for "Hello" and four for "Goodnight". But five meant "Come over as soon as possible because I've got something important to reveal."

"Well in that case, you'd better go over. But make sure that you are back here in ten minutes," said Marilla.

Anne was true to her word and returned in time. "Oh Marilla, it was important news," she cried. "As you know, it's Diana's birthday tomorrow. And you'll never guess – her mother says she wants me to stay with her tomorrow night! Her cousins are coming in a sleigh and we're all going off to a concert in the Avonlea Hall."

Marilla wasn't very happy with the idea. She felt Anne might get too excited, or even catch a fever.

"Please! Please! Please!" begged Anne.

Matthew thought Anne should go, so Marilla finally gave in.

"But don't blame me if you catch your death

of cold through being in that old hall and sleeping in a chilly bedroom at the Barry's house," she grumbled.

The next day at school, there was nothing talked about except the concert. Anne hardly noticed that Gilbert had beaten her in spelling and arithmetic.

The real excitement began just after school. Anne had tea at Diana's house and then went upstairs to change for the concert.

Diana did Anne's hair in a new style and Anne tied special bows in Diana's. Then they dressed, their eyes glowing with excitement.

The next thing they heard was the jangling of sleigh bells. It was Diana's cousins arriving.

Anne had never seen anything so marvelous as that sleigh. Diana and Anne climbed aboard and then they were off, riding across the smooth snow into a magnificent sunset.

The frosty air echoed to the sounds of tinkling sleigh bells and happy laughter.

And how Anne enjoyed the concert! She had never heard so many different songs sung by so many people. But there was one song she didn't listen to.

Anne had found a book lying under her seat before the concert began. She decided to read it while Gilbert sang his song. And as everyone else clapped madly when he finished, Anne just sat reading.

It was past eleven o'clock by the time they got home. "Anne," said Diana, as they crept into the house, "I don't know how you could read a book when Gilbert was singing. He was so good."

"Diana," replied Anne, with all the dignity she could manage, "you are my best friend but even so, I can't allow you to speak of *that* person in front of me!"

Diana just laughed.

"Come on," said Anne. "I'll race you to the bedroom!"

They ran up the stairs and took a short cut through the spare room. There, they tried to leap across the bed in one go. Instead, they landed in the middle.

Something moved beneath them. There was a gasp. "Merciful goodness!" a voice cried out.

Anne and Diana screamed, leapt off the bed and escaped to their own bedroom.

"Who or what was that?" cried Anne, almost out of breath with excitement and shock.

"I completely forgot," laughed Diana. "It was Father's Great Aunt Josephine. She's

Riding across the smooth snow

awfully old; at least seventy. She's staying with us. She's dreadfully prim and proper. We'll be in big trouble in the morning."

The two girls couldn't worry about it at that moment. They were too busy giggling.

Something moved beneath them.

Chapter 21
Great Aunt Josephine

The next morning there was no sign of Great Aunt Josephine. Mrs. Barry smiled at the girls and asked them whether they had a good time at the concert.

The two little angels smiled back. They thought they had got away with the mischief of the night before. Perhaps Josephine thought that she had dreamed two girls jumped on her bed in the middle of the night.

It was only later in the day when Anne met Diana by the orchard that she heard what trouble they had caused.

"Great Aunt Josephine was fairly dancing with rage when she came downstairs," giggled Diana. "She said I was the worst-behaved girl she had ever met, and that my parents should be ashamed of the way they brought me up. She says she won't stay a day longer."

"Oh dear," said Anne, trying not to laugh. "What do your parents think about all this?"

"That's the problem," explained Diana. "Great Aunt Josephine is very rich and I think she was going to give all her money to Mother and Father when she died. I don't think she will now. They're very annoyed with me."

"Why didn't you tell them it was my fault?" asked Anne. "It was me who suggested we race to our bedroom."

"As if I would!" said Diana. "I'm no telltale. Anyway, I was as much to blame as you."

"Well, I'm going to tell her," said Anne.

"You can't," cried Diana. "She'll eat you alive!"

"She can't frighten me any more than I'm already frightened," said Anne. "It was my fault and I've got to confess. Fortunately, I've had plenty of practice at confessing."

And so it was agreed. They walked back to the Barry home. Great Aunt Josephine was in the sitting room. Anne knocked on the door.

"Come in!" snapped Great Aunt Josephine.

Anne slowly opened the door. Miss Josephine Barry, thin, prim and rigid, was knitting fiercely by the fire. There was a ferocious look on her face as her gold-rimmed spectacles rose up and down with each stitch she made.

She wheeled around in her chair to face

Great Aunt Josephine

Anne knocked on the door.

Anne. "And who are you?" she asked coldly.

"I'm Anne of Green Gables and I've come to confess."

"Confess what?" asked the old woman.

"That it was my fault we jumped on you in bed last night. Diana would never have thought of doing such a thing. It was me who said we should race to bed. Diana is very ladylike, Miss Barry. So you must see how unjust it is to blame her."

"Oh is it, young miss," said Great Aunt Josephine. "I rather think Diana did her share of the jumping. Such carryings-on in a respectable house!"

"I think you should forgive us, Miss Barry. Or at least forgive Diana. If you must be cross, be cross with me. I am so used to people being cross with me that one more person won't matter. I can endure people being cross with me better than Diana can."

The angry look went out of the old woman's eyes.

"Little girls never did this sort of thing when I was young," she said, a thin smile playing around her lips. "You don't know what it is like to be awakened out of a deep sleep by two girls bouncing on you."

"I must admit I don't," said Anne, "but I can imagine it. It must have been very disturbing. But you must see our side too. Have you any imagination, Miss Barry? If you have, put yourself in our place. When we jumped on the bed, you nearly scared us to death."

Miss Josephine Barry had to laugh at this. "I'm afraid my imagination is a bit rusty," she said. "It's so long since I used it. Now come and sit beside me and tell me about yourself."

Anne said she was terribly sorry but she didn't have the time. "My duty is to go home to Miss Marilla Cuthbert and help make dinner," she said. "She is a very kind lady who saved me from the orphanage and looked after me. She is bringing me up. She is doing her best, but it can be hard work with me. I'm so naughty sometimes. So please don't blame her if my behavior hasn't been the best. It is my fault."

With that said, Anne begged Great Aunt Josephine to forgive Diana and stay and leave all her money to Mr. and Mrs. Barry.

The old woman laughed and said she would, as long as Anne came and visited her now and again.

Great Aunt Josephine ended up staying for a month, and made good friends with Anne.

Begging Great Aunt Josephine to forgive Diana

Great Aunt Josephine

When she finally went home, she invited Anne to come and stay with her. "I'll put you in my spare room, but don't expect me to come a-jumping on you in the middle of the night," she said.

Chapter 22
Ghosts, Green Hair and Horse Medicine

Marilla couldn't believe how fast Anne was growing up. She was eleven years old when she first came to Green Gables. Now she was about to have her fourteenth birthday. "Oh, how the months and years pass so quickly," she sighed.

Anne may have been growing older, but she still managed to get into lots of trouble.

One day she tried to walk along the ridge of the kitchen roof at Green Gables, on a dare from one her friends. She lost her balance and tumbled to the ground, and broke an ankle!

Anne was off school for several weeks. She worried the whole time that Gilbert might get ahead of her in his lessons, while she was away.

When the ankle had mended, Anne soon found herself in more trouble.

She came home one day and told Marilla she

had been walking in Haunted Wood.

Marilla had never heard of any wood with that name and asked her where it was.

"It's where the fir trees are by the brook," explained Anne. "I've told all my friends that I'm positive it's haunted.

"Fiddlesticks!" said Marilla. "That wood is not haunted. You just imagined it is. You shouldn't try to scare people."

"It *is* haunted!" cried Anne. "I'm sure there are ghosts down there."

"In that case," said Marilla, with a frown, "we'll have to find a way to prove to you that there's no such thing as ghosts."

Marilla decided to make Anne walk alone through the wood one evening. "That'll cure your imagination," she said. "You'll see that the wood isn't haunted at all and it will be the end of this nonsense."

Anne didn't want to go, but Marilla insisted. On that walk, Anne imagined goblins lurking in every shadow. She saw ghostly hands reaching out to grasp her at every step. Two old tree trunks rubbing together in the wind wailed out like an angry ghost. Bats swooped in the darkness.

When Anne got home she was shaking with

fright. Marilla asked her if any ghosts had caught her.

"No, Marilla, I'll b-b-be h-h-happy to call it Happy Wood in future," she stuttered.

But the next morning, Anne realized that Marilla had been right. The wood wasn't haunted at all. It was just her imagination at work.

Anne's next adventure happened when the church minister came to tea. Somehow, she managed to put horse liniment in the cake she baked, instead of rose water. The Minister's wife thought it all very funny and forgave Anne.

On another occasion, Marilla had trouble getting Anne out of bed in time for school. The girl hid beneath the bedclothes and refused to come out

Marilla eventually pulled back the bed-clothes and was shocked to see that Anne's hair had turned green all over.

Anne had bought some hair dye from a traveling salesman, thinking it would turn her red hair dark brown. It had gone badly wrong and green was the result.

Before she went back to school, Anne cut all her hair off and told her friends she had an

Bats swooped in the darkness.

illness. But her bright red locks soon grew back.

Next came trouble on Barry's Pond. Anne had been playing with Diana, Ruby Gillis and Jane Andrews, on a small raft they had built. Of course, it had to be Anne who floated out into the middle of the pond just as the raft began to sink.

The other girls rushed off to find help. And while they were away, who should come to the rescue in his own boat? It was none other than Anne's sworn enemy, Gilbert Blythe.

Gilbert grabbed Anne, seconds before the raft broke up. He tried to make friends with Anne that day. He even told her that her hair was beautiful. But still Anne refused to forgive him.

Later, Diana told Anne that Gilbert had done the most romantic thing by rescuing her. Anne was as obstinate as ever. "No," she said, "Gilbert and I can never be friends."

Anne certainly learned some lessons with all her mistakes and accidents.

"The haunted wood cured me of letting my imagination run away with me," she told Matthew. "The horse liniment cured me of careless cooking. Dyeing my hair cured me of vanity.

Gilbert rescues Anne

Anne of Green Gables

And being saved from drowning by Gilbert has cured me of romance."

Matthew took hold of Anne's hand and gave her some advice. "Don't give up completely on romance," he said. "A little of it is a good thing."

Romance! Huh! Anne and Diana had already promised each other they would never marry.

They agreed that they would grow up as old maids and live together forever.

But secretly they both dreamed of meeting some handsome, dashing young man.

Chapter 23
Matthew's Christmas Present

One Christmas, Anne and all her school friends decided to put on a concert. They usually rehearsed in the kitchen at Green Gables, where Matthew would listen to them.

One evening, he spotted something. Somehow, Anne was different to all the other girls. He wasn't sure how at first. But then it hit him.

Marilla had always dressed Anne in plain, dark dresses, all made to exactly the same pattern. The other girls wore colorful dresses of red, blue, pink and white.

More than that, Matthew had often heard Anne talking about how she wished her dresses had fashionable puffs on the sleeves, like the ones the other girls wore.

Matthew had an idea. Christmas was only two weeks away. What better time to buy Anne a special dress? The very next day he rode off to town to do some shopping. This was to be his secret. He wouldn't even tell Marilla.

Now shopping was not something Matthew liked to do. He was very shy when it came to talking to the sales assistants.

The idea of buying a girl's dress was more that a matter of shyness. The thought of having to ask for a dress terrified him.

He crept into Samuel Lawson's general store. Before he could even look around, Miss Lucilla Harris, Mr. Lawson's beautiful young sales assistant, descended on him.

"Hello Mr. Cuthbert. What can I do for you today?" she asked.

"Have you any ... any ... any ... any ..." stammered Matthew, absolutely unable to get the word dress out of his mouth.

"Have you any ... any ... any garden rakes?" he blurted out, all of a sudden.

Lucilla went away and returned with a rake. "Anything else, Mr. Cuthbert?" she asked.

"Er ... yes ... have you got any ..." Still the word *dresses* wouldn't come out. "... any ... any hayseed?"

By the time Matthew had finished his shopping he had a rake, some hayseed, a rat trap, and several other small items – but no dress. He escaped from the shop and rode home.

In desperation, he went and asked Rachel to

Matthew's Christmas Present

The sales assistant descended on him.

go and buy him a dress for Anne. Rachel was delighted to be let in on the secret, and did not fail him.

And so, Christmas Eve came at last. Snow fell all night. When Anne awoke the next day the ground was completely covered. She went downstairs to breakfast.

"Merry Christmas Marilla! Merry Christmas Matthew!" she said. "I'm so glad it snowed. Any other kind of Christmas wouldn't seem real, would it? I don't like green Christmases."

Matthew sheepishly passed his parcel to Anne. She unwrapped it in an instant, and found her dress.

"Oh, Matthew," she cried. "How wonderful!"

The dress was a lovely soft brown color, with dainty frills and a waist tucked in, in the fashionable way. But the sleeves were the crowning glory. They had beautiful puffs.

"Do you like it?" asked Matthew.

"Like it?" she replied. "It's perfectly exquisite! I can never thank you enough. Look at those lovely sleeves. It seems to me this must be a happy dream."

Marilla, who was just as surprised as Anne to see the dress, wasn't so sure. "I don't think you really needed another dress," she said, "but

"It's perfectly exquisite!"

seeing as Matthew has got you one, look after it."

The next moment there was a knock at the door and Diana burst in with another present for Anne – a pair of soft, warm slippers.

"Oh, I am dreaming," said Anne. "This is a wonderful Christmas."

The concert that night was a great success too. After Anne had gone to bed, Marilla and Matthew sat talking.

"I was very proud of Anne at the concert tonight," admitted Marilla, "but I didn't tell her so. I don't want her to get big ideas about herself."

"Well, Marilla," said Matthew, "I was so proud of her that I had to tell her before she went to bed."

"I'm glad you did," said Marilla.

Poor Marilla could never quite express her feelings. So she was happy Matthew had.

And so a perfect Christmas ended.

Chapter 24
Examinations

After Christmas, it was time for more hard work at school. Marilla and Matthew also had to decide what Anne should do when she left Avonlea School.

There was a new teacher at school that term. Her name was Miss Stacey. Anne loved Miss Stacey – she was exactly the opposite kind of person to stern old Mr. Phillips.

Miss Stacey saw what a clever girl Anne was. She suggested that Anne should try to win a place at Queen's Teaching Academy, to train as a teacher.

"But won't that be too expensive?" Anne asked Marilla.

"It will be expensive to go to Queen's," said Marilla, "but we promised to bring you up and give you the best education we could. You'll always have a home here at Green Gables. But we think you should go to Queen's if you pass the exam."

Marilla looked at Anne with a big smile on her face. "Though how you'll ever become a teacher, I don't know," she said. "It's a marvel your tongue isn't worn out already!"

Miss Stacy organized a special class for the pupils who would be trying for a place at Queen's. It included Jane Andrews, Ruby Gillis and Gilbert Blythe.

The saddest thing for Anne was that Diana Barry's parents didn't want their daughter to go to Queen's.

Anne did look forward to continuing her rivalry with Gilbert. But the strange thing about it all was that because she had ignored Gilbert for so long, he now ignored her. And she didn't like it at all.

In fact, she discovered that she didn't really dislike him any more. Anne realized that she had forgiven and forgotten, without knowing it.

How she wished she could be friendly with him now.

There were quite a lot of things Anne was learning about life.

One evening she was sitting with Marilla, talking about Rachel.

"Do you know, I do try to be good," said Anne, "but somehow, whenever I'm with

Examinations

A special class.

Rachel I feel desperately wicked and do the very things she tells me I shouldn't do. Why do I feel that? Am I all bad?"

"If you're bad," was Marilla's surprising reply, "then I'm bad too. She has the same effect on me."

Later that night, when Anne had gone to bed, Marilla spoke with Matthew.

"I'm going to miss Anne terribly if she gets to Queen's," she sighed."

And Matthew heartily agreed with her.

*

Anne, her friends and Gilbert studied hard. They sat the Queen's exams and then had a nervous wait, to see how they'd done. To their delight, each of them won a place!

Matthew and Marilla were so proud of their young orphan, especially as she shared equal top marks with Gilbert.

For Anne, the hardest thing was leaving Avonlea School and her beloved Diana.

Two big tears rolled down Diana's face as Anne emptied her desk for the last time. "I'll never find another desk-mate like you," she said.

"I'm going to miss you terribly, Diana," said Anne, giving her best friend a hug.

"I'll never find another desk-mate like you."

Chapter 25
Farewells

There was a big farewell concert at Avonlea Hall for the pupils who were going on to Queen's.

Anne was to sing a song. So many people turned up that she got stage fright for the first time in her life.

Then she saw Gilbert sitting at the back of the hall. She noticed that he had a smile on his face. In reality, the smile was there because he was admiring Anne in her pretty dress. But all Anne saw was a rival, taunting her with a smile.

It was all Anne needed to get rid of her stage fright. She would not fail in front of Gilbert Blythe!

She took a deep breath and flung her head back proudly. She gave the performance of her life and the audience burst into loud applause at the end. Diana clapped louder than anyone. Marilla and Matthew were so proud of her, too.

Farewells

Giving the performance of her life

That night, Anne sat with Marilla and Matthew in the kitchen at Green Gables.

Anne saw a tear in Marilla's eye and asked her why she was crying.

"Oh, it's nothing," said Marilla. "I can't help thinking of the little girl you used to be. I was wishing you could have stayed a little girl, even if you were to keep getting up to mischief. But you've grown up now and soon you'll be going away. Soon you won't belong to Avonlea at all."

"Marilla," said Anne, moving over and slipping into Marilla's lap, "I haven't changed at all, not really. I've only pruned down and branched out a bit. The real *me* is just the same. It doesn't make any difference where I go or how much I change outwardly. At heart I shall always be your little Anne, who will love you and Matthew, and dear Green Gables more and more, every day of my life."

Anne laid her fresh young cheek against Marilla's faded one and reached out to lay a hand on Matthew's shoulder.

It was too much for Matthew. Tears were now filling his eyes and he had to get up, and go for a walk in the garden.

In the cool air outside, warm thoughts tumbled around his head.

"Oh what a blessing that little girl has been to us," he said to himself. "Never was there a luckier mistake than when that little boy turned out to be a girl. Mind you, I don't believe it was luck. Someone, somewhere, knew we needed her and she needed us."

And so the day finally came for Anne to leave for Queen's. There were tearful farewells with Marilla, Matthew and Diana, who all came into town with Anne to say goodbye at the station.

That night, Marilla lay in bed and thought about the empty room down the corridor. Then she turned over and buried her face in the pillow, and sobbed for the girl who was no longer there.

Alone in her bedroom at Queen's, Anne cried for Marilla, Matthew and Diana.

Tearful farewells

Chapter 26
At Queen's

In the weeks that followed at Queen's, Anne's homesickness at being away from Green Gables did start to wear off. Besides, she was allowed home on some weekends. She took the train with Jane Andrews, Ruby Gillis and Gilbert Blythe.

Diana and several other Avonlea young folks were always waiting to meet them at the station, and walk the rest of the way home.

Gilbert used to walk with Ruby Gillis and carry her bags. Ruby had grown into a very pretty young lady. She wore long skirts and had her hair pinned up.

Jane Andrews didn't think that Ruby was the sort of girl Gilbert would like. Anne didn't think so either, although she would never have said so.

She couldn't help thinking now what a pleasant friend Gilbert might have made. Anne saw that they had similar interests . . .

books, studying, and ambitions for the future.

Anne imagined what interesting conversations she would have if Gilbert carried her bags.

Back at Queen's, her rivalry with Gilbert was as intense as ever during classes. But now Anne showed no bitterness to him. She was challenging Gilbert as a worthy foe. And he recognized that.

Another person who recognized Anne's worth was Great Aunt Josephine Barry. She lived near Queen's and Anne went to see her now and again.

"Young Anne," she would say, "your character has as many shades as a rainbow, and every shade is the prettiest while it lasts."

*

The term at Queen's ended with examinations. There were two top examination prizes to be won. The first was the Queen's Silver medal. The top schools in the area always tried to get the winner of that medal to teach in their school.

The second, and ultimate, prize was the Queen's Scholarship. This gave the winner the chance to go on to study at a top college, rather than start teaching straight away.

At Queen's

Walking home from Avonlea station

With examinations over, the long wait for the results began. But Anne was just happy to get back to Avonlea.

Four weeks later, Anne, Jane, Ruby and Gilbert returned to Queen's to find out their results.

There were dozens of people in the school hall, looking up and down the lists of names on several notice boards. At first, Anne couldn't see her name anywhere.

Gilbert Blythe quickly spotted his. He had won the Silver Medal for his work. Anne saw all his friends congratulating him. She felt that he had won the battle between them. Surely he would take the Queen's Scholarship prize, too.

Suddenly, a great shriek went up. It was Jane's voice. "Anne! Anne! Quick! Look here!"

Anne ran across to the large main notice board. She couldn't believe it. Her name was there. And beside it were two words:

Queen's Scholar.

Anne had won the scholarship!

All the girls crowded around to congratulate her, pushing and hugging her. All Anne could think of was how proud Marilla and Matthew would be.

And they certainly were when, a few days later, they attended the prize-giving ceremony.

When Anne climbed onto the stage to accept her prize, Matthew whispered to Marilla. "Do you want to swap her for a boy now? I reckon you're glad you kept her now, eh?"

"Matthew Cuthbert!" laughed Marilla, in mock anger. "Will you ever stop teasing me over that?"

Anne had won the scholarship!

"Don't expect so," smiled Matthew, a tear coming to his eye as Anne walked down from the stage.

That evening, Anne returned to Green Gables with Matthew and Marilla.

The apple blossom was out and, for Anne, the world felt fresh and new again.

Diana was at Green Gables to meet her. "Oh, Diana," said Anne, "it's so good to be back home again!"

At breakfast the next morning, Anne noticed how gray-faced and unwell Matthew had become.

Later she asked Marilla if Matthew was all right.

"No," she answered. "He's had some trouble with his heart. I've been very worried about him. I'm hoping he'll improve now you're home. You always cheer him up."

Anne went for a walk with Matthew, as the sun set that evening. "Matthew, why don't you take things easier?" she asked.

"I've always worked hard," he answered. "I'll be like an old horse and die with my harness on."

"If only I'd been a boy," said Anne. "I could help you with the heavy work."

With Matthew and Marilla

"I'd rather have you than a dozen boys," said Matthew affectionately. "What boy would have won the Queen's Scholarship? No, that was my own little girl, and the girl I'm most proud of in this world."

Matthew smiled his shy smile at Anne when they got back to Green Gables and went inside.

Anne took the memory of that smile to her room that night. She sat for a long time at the window, dreaming of the future. The moon was up and the frogs were singing by the brook.

Anne always remembered the silvery beauty and fragrant calm of that night.

It was the last night before tragedy stepped into her life.

Chapter 27
A Terrible Sadness

Anne and Marilla were returning to Green Gables the next morning after picking wildflowers, when they saw Matthew in the porch doorway.

He looked at them with a strange smile on his face. It was as if he was saying goodbye to his best friends.

Then Matthew sank gently to the ground.

Marilla and Anne threw their flowers aside and ran to him. It was too late. Matthew's kind old heart had given up at last.

On that sad day, everyone from Avonlea came to say farewell to Matthew.

Diana came over too, and asked Anne if she wanted to stay with her that night.

Anne thanked Diana, but said she must be with Marilla. "It's so hard to imagine that Matthew has gone forever," she said. "Only last night we were talking together and he told me how proud he was of me. Now I can't say

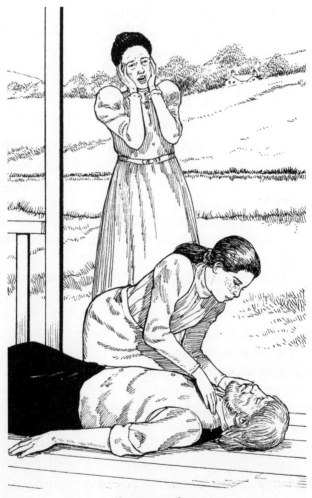

It was too late.

anything to him ever again."

That night, the tears that Anne had held back all day finally came. She sobbed her heart out. Marilla heard her and came to her bedroom. She sat on the bed beside Anne.

"Oh, Marilla, what will we do without Matthew?" sobbed Anne.

"We have each other," said Marilla. "And I certainly wouldn't know what to do without you."

For the first time in her life, Marilla poured out her love for Anne.

"I know I've been strict and harsh with you sometimes," she began, "but you mustn't think I didn't love you as much as Matthew. It's never been easy for me to speak from my heart, but at times like this it's easier. I love you as dearly as if you were my own flesh and blood. You've been my joy and comfort ever since you came to Green Gables."

Deep down Anne had always known it. But now she knew for sure. The two of them fell into each other's arms.

*

Two days later they laid Matthew Cuthbert to rest. Anne planted a rose on his grave.

Planting a rose on Matthew's grave

A Terrible Sadness

That evening, Marilla and Anne sat alone together at Green Gables, talking about the future.

"That boy Gilbert is going to become a teacher, isn't he?" asked Marilla.

"I think so," answered Anne.

"He's a nice looking fellow," said Marilla, "just like his father."

"What was Gilbert's father like?" asked Anne.

"Kind. Intelligent. We were real good friends, he and I," sighed Marilla, her mind seeming to drift away into the past for a moment. "People always said he was my boyfriend."

"What happened between you?" said Anne, suddenly appearing very interested.

"We had a quarrel and I wouldn't forgive him. Well, like you, by the time I was ready to forgive him it was too late. He never came back to me. "

Anne was fascinated. "So you did have a bit of romance in your life, too?"

"Yes, you might call it that," said Marilla shyly. "Everyone has forgotten about me and John Blythe. Yet we might have become husband and wife. It was seeing Gilbert the other day that brought it all back to me."

Anne thought how sad it was. Although she had been happy with her brother Matthew most of her life, Marilla might have married and had children.

But if the facts about Marilla's romance came as a surprise, there was an even bigger one for Anne just around the corner.

Chapter 28

For the Love of Green Gables

"Sell Green Gables! You can't!" cried Anne.

Marilla was in tears when she gave Anne the news. They would have to sell their home and farm if they were to survive after Matthew's death.

It came as a terrible shock to Anne.

"Oh, Anne, I wish I didn't have to," sobbed Marilla, "but I can't stay here alone. I can't run the farm and we haven't enough money. It's all got to be sold."

Anne went back to her bedroom to think about the news. She imagined Marilla dying of loneliness in some faraway town. The idea was just too terrible to bear.

Then Anne had an idea. And the more she thought about it, the better it seemed . . .

Early the next morning, Anne went over to Diana's place. An hour later, she came running back to Green Gables and went to see Marilla, who was in the kitchen.

"You are not going to sell Green Gables, or the farm!" Anne announced, almost out of breath. "And you won't have to stay here alone, either."

Marilla was completely confused. "What do you mean?"

"I decided that I'm not going to take up the scholarship I won at Queen's," said Anne proudly. "I couldn't leave you now. I'm going to get a job as a teacher somewhere near here, perhaps in Charlottetown. I can ride there and back in the buggy each day. They tell me that Gilbert Blythe has already been asked to become the teacher at Avonlea School."

"But the debts," said Marilla. "I have to sell Green Gables to pay those. Nothing can change that."

"Yes, it can," said Anne. "I've just come from Diana's. Her father wants to rent your land. That will pay off the debts and give you enough to live on."

Marilla was astounded. "But Anne, you can't give up your scholarship. That's your future. You can't sacrifice that for me."

"Yes I can!" cried Anne. "Nothing would be worse than giving up Green Gables. Nothing would hurt me more. My mind is made up,

"You are not going to sell Green Gables!"

Marilla. You'll never be lonesome. And we'll be very comfortable and happy here together, you and I."

"I don't think I should let you give up your scholarship," repeated Marilla.

"You can't stop me!" Anne laughed cheekily. "I'm now almost sixteen and still as obstinate as a mule. And besides, I can study all the things I want to at home. So don't feel sorry for me. My heart is glad at the thought of staying here. Nobody could love Green Gables like you and I do . . . so we must keep it."

"You blessed girl!" said Marilla, tears coming into her eyes. "I give in. But I'll make it up to you somehow."

Just then, Rachel arrived at Green Gables with some extraordinary news. "The governors of Avonlea School have decided," she announced importantly, "that Anne is to be the new teacher at Avonlea."

"It can't be so," gasped Anne. "They've already given the job to Gilbert Blythe."

"They did give him the job," explained Rachel. "But Gilbert knew how you wanted to stay with Marilla. So he stood down and suggested to the governors that you should be teacher. He's found another job in Charlottetown."

For the Love of Green Gables

Rachel has some extraordinary news

Anne was silent for several moments. "I don't think Gilbert should sacrifice his job at the Avonlea School for me," she said.

"I guess you can't refuse," smiled Rachel. "Gilbert has already signed the papers for his job at the school in Charlottetown."

Chapter 29

Time to Forgive

That evening, Anne went to Avonlea Church to put fresh flowers on Matthew's grave, and to water the rose she had planted. She loved the peace and quiet of the place.

She lingered there until dusk and then walked down to the Lake of Shining Waters. It was past sunset and below her, bathed in the warm afterglow of the sun, lay Avonlea. Lights from the houses twinkled across the valley.

The beauty of it all thrilled Anne's heart. "Dear old world," she whispered to herself, "you are very lovely and I'm glad to be alive in you."

She was halfway down the hill and near the Blythe homestead, when a tall lad came whistling out of the gate.

The whistle died on Gilbert Blythe's lips as he recognized Anne. He lifted his cap politely and would have passed on if Anne hadn't held out her hand.

"Gilbert," she said, with blushing cheeks, "I want to thank you for giving up the job at Avonlea School for me. It was very, very good and kind of you. I want you to know just how much I appreciate it."

"It wasn't particularly good of me," was the reply. "I was pleased to be able to do a small thing to help you and Marilla. And if it helps to make us friends after all these years, all the better. Am I forgiven for what I said to you so long ago?"

Anne smiled. "I should have forgiven you years ago. What a stubborn little goose I am."

"We were born to be good friends," said Gilbert. "And I know we can help each other in so many ways. And right now, I shall walk you home. It's getting dark."

Marilla looked curiously at Anne when she came in. "Wasn't that Gilbert I saw walking you home? I thought you were old enemies."

"We were," laughed Anne. "But we decided we would both be a lot happier if we were friends instead."

Marilla smiled. She had never seen Anne so happy.

That night, Anne sat at her bedroom window and looked out across the valley. A breeze

"I want to thank you."

purred through her hair and the stars twinkled in the moonlit heavens.

For a moment she thought of Matthew. Perhaps he was out there somewhere. She remembered his last words to her again . . . *"my own little girl – the girl I'm most proud of in this world."*

Anne didn't cry now. She was thinking of the future and the job of teaching at Avonlea School, and looking after Marilla as she got

Thinking of the future

older. It was what Matthew would have wanted her to do.

On the other side of the valley, Anne saw a light flicker on and off. She realized what was happening. She counted the flickers. It was four. It was Diana saying goodnight.

Anne hurriedly lit the candle in her window and signaled four flashes back to her friend.

Then she sat back and looked up at the stars again.

"God's in his heaven," she whispered, softly, "and all's well with the world."

The End

Black Beauty

By Anna Sewell

Born on a sunlit meadow in an English village,
Black Beauty has a happy upbringing and a
wonderful home, with a kind and caring master.

Then the beautiful young horse is sold and
separated from his friends.

So begins an extraordinary journey through life
for Black Beauty; a journey that brings moments
of triumph and joy, as well as pain, suffering,
loneliness and cruelty at the hands of others.

Can Black Beauty ever find true happiness again?
Will he find his way back to the peaceful
meadows of his youth? Or is he condemned to
live in misery for the rest of his life, like so many
working horses of his time.

Black Beauty is one of the most moving animal
stories ever told.

Lorna Doone

By R.D. Blackmore

Lorna Doone is a romantic adventure that has thrilled generations of young readers.

This famous tale of seventeenth century England is set on Exmoor, a wild and lawless land terrorized by the dreaded Doones.

At the heart of the story are John Ridd, a brave young farmer, sworn to avenge his father's murder by the Doones and Carver Doone, a brutal, aristocratic outlaw and killer. The there is Lorna Doone—the mysterious, dark-eyed beauty who both men would die for.

But who is Lorna Doone? Who were her mother and father? And can John Ridd finally discover her true identity?

The Call of the Wild

By Jack London

When the pale moon rises over the Klondike River and the night wolves run, you can still hear the lonely howl of Buck, the most famous ghost dog of them all.

Generations of readers have thrilled to the adventures of big-hearted Buck. Kidnapped, cruelly beaten and starved, he becomes a legend when he is shipped to the snowy northlands to work as a sled dog on the goldfields.

Buck's companions have become almost as famous. There's Spitz, the dog that Buck must fight for the leadership of the pack, the one-eyed Sol-leks, the tragic Curly, Dave, Joe, Pike, Dub and Dolly. And there's John Thornton, the man who Buck comes to love like no other master.

Yet, Buck knows that one day he must leave the human world, for his ancestors are telling him to answer the call of the wild.

The Secret Garden

By Frances Hodgson Burnett

Mary Lennox is an ill-tempered and
spoilt little girl.

When both her parents die, she is sent to live with
her sad uncle in a rambling old manor house.

At first, Mary hates the manor house. But in the
grounds she discovers a mysterious garden that
has been locked up for ten years.

Even more mysteriously, she meets Colin, a sickly
boy who has been hidden from the world since
the garden was locked.

Mary and Colin, and their friend Dickon—an
amazing boy who can charm wild animals—help
the secret garden to come alive again.

And as the garden blooms once more, its special
magic brings happiness to everyone in the
unhappy old house.

The Time Machine

By H.G. Wells

In 1890 a Victorian scientist tells his friends he has
built a Time Machine that will take him far into
the future.

His friends don't believe him. But then the man
vanishes.

The Time Traveler eventually returns to tell his
friends that he has journeyed nearly a million
years into the future, to the year 802,701.

He reveals how he discovers a new race of human
beings called the Eloi. They seem to enjoy a
perfect life of leisure and enjoyment.

But the nightmarish truth only emerges when the
Time Traveler meets the Morlocks, a dread
underworld race of creatures.

H.G. Wells' vision of the future and the Time
Traveler's extraordinary adventures create a
terrifying masterpiece of science fiction.

The Wizard of Oz

By L. F. Baum

The Wizard of Oz is the famous children's story that became one of the most popular movies ever made.

Farm girl Dorothy and her dog Toto are magically carried away from their Kansas home to the mysterious Land of Oz.

As millions of children around the world know, Dorothy must follow the yellow brick road if she is ever to get home again. On her journey she meets the Scarecrow who wants a brain, the Tin Man who wants a heart, the Cowardly Lion who wants some courage and of course, the very mysterious Wizard of Oz.

This enchanting story delights at every step along the yellow brick road.

Treasure Island

By Robert Louis Stevenson

The one-legged Long John Silver, treacherous Captain Billy Bones, wicked Black Dog and the terrifying Blind Pew … they were the cruelest and most frightening pirates ever to sail the high seas.

They all dreamed of finding Captain Flint's buried treasure.

But it was young Jim Hawkins, just 14 years old, who found Flint's map of Treasure Island.

Could he and his friends outwit those bloodthirsty pirates? And what secrets lay with Ben Gunn, the wild man of the island?

Robert Louis Stevenson's classic story, which has thrilled generations of younger readers, is the most famous pirate adventure of them all.